'She decided she would teach him to speak and he was very soon able to say, "Pretty boy!", "Your servant, sir!" and "Hail Mary!"'

GUSTAVE FLAUBERT
Born 1821, Rouen, France
Died 1880, Croisset, France

This story was first published in its original French
in Gustave Flaubert's *Trois Contes* in 1877,
translated as *Three Tales*.

FLAUBERT IN PENGUIN CLASSICS
Madame Bovary
Sentimental Education
Three Tales
Salammbo

GUSTAVE FLAUBERT

A Simple Heart

Translated by
Roger Whitehouse

PENGUIN BOOKS

PENGUIN CLASSICS

UK | USA | Canada | Ireland | Australia
India | New Zealand | South Africa

Penguin Books is part of the Penguin Random House group of companies
whose addresses can be found at global.penguinrandomhouse.com.

Penguin
Random House
UK

This edition published in Penguin Classics 2015
004

Set in 9.5/13 pt Baskerville 10 Pro
Typeset by Jouve (UK), Milton Keynes
Printed in Great Britain by Clays Ltd, St Ives plc

A CIP catalogue record for this book is available from the British Library

ISBN: 978–0–141–39750–4

www.greenpenguin.co.uk

A Simple Heart

1

For half a century, Madame Aubain's housemaid Félicité was the envy of all the good ladies of Pont-l'Evêque.

For just one hundred francs a year, she did all the cooking and the housework, she saw to the darning, the washing and the ironing, she could bridle a horse, keep the chickens well fed and churn the butter. What is more she remained faithful to her mistress, who, it must be said, was not the easiest of people to get on with.

Madame Aubain had married a handsome but impecunious young man, who had died at the beginning of 1809, leaving her with two very young children and substantial debts. Upon his death, she sold her properties, with the exception of the two farms at Toucques and Geffosses, which between them provided her with an income of no more than five thousand francs in rent, and she moved out of her house in Saint-Melaine to live in another which was less costly to maintain, which had belonged to her family and which was situated behind the market.

This house had a slate roof and stood between an alley

and a narrow street leading down to the river. Inside, the floors were at different levels, making it very easy to trip up. A narrow hallway separated the kitchen from the living room in which Madame Aubain remained all day long, sitting in a wicker armchair close to the casement window. Against the wainscoting, which was painted white, there stood a row of eight mahogany chairs. A barometer hung on the wall above an old piano, piled high with a pyramid-shaped assortment of packets and cardboard boxes. Two easy chairs upholstered in tapestry stood on either side of a Louis-Quinze-style mantelpiece in yellow marble. The clock, in the middle, was designed to look like a Temple of Vesta, and the whole room smelt musty, due to the fact that the floor level was lower than the garden.

On the first floor, there was 'Madame's' bedroom, a very large room, decorated with pale, flowery wallpaper and containing a picture of 'Monsieur' dressed up in the fanciful attire that was fashionable at the time. This room led directly to a smaller bedroom which housed two children's beds, each with the mattress removed. Next came the parlour, which was always kept locked and was full of furniture draped in dust-sheets. Finally, there was a corridor leading to a study; books and papers lay stacked on the shelves of a bookcase which ran around three walls of the room and surrounded a large writing-desk in dark wood. The two end panels of this bookcase were covered in line drawings, landscapes in gouache and etchings by

Audran, a reminder of better days and of more expensive tastes that were now a thing of the past. On the second floor was Félicité's bedroom, lit by a dormer window which looked out over the fields.

Félicité always rose at first light to make sure she was in time for mass, and then worked without a break until the evening. As soon as dinner was finished, the crockery cleared away and the door firmly bolted, she would cover the log fire with ashes and go to sleep in front of the fireplace, holding her rosary in her hand. No one could have been more persistent when it came to haggling over prices and, as for cleanliness, the spotless state of her saucepans was the despair of all the other serving maids in Pont-l'Evêque. She wasted nothing and ate slowly, gathering every crumb of her loaf from the table with her fingers, a twelve-pound loaf baked especially for her and which lasted her twenty days.

In all weathers she wore a printed kerchief fastened behind with a pin, a bonnet which completely covered her hair, grey stockings, a red skirt and over her jacket a bibbed apron like those worn by hospital nurses.

Her face was thin and her voice was shrill. At twenty-five, people took her to be as old as forty. After her fiftieth birthday, it became impossible to say what age she was at all. She hardly ever spoke, and her upright stance and deliberate movements gave her the appearance of a woman made out of wood, driven as if by clockwork.

2

Like other girls, she had once fallen in love.

Her father, a stonemason by trade, had been killed falling from some scaffolding. Following this, her mother died and her sisters went their separate ways. A farmer took her in and, even though she was still a very young girl, he would send her out into the fields to look after the cows. She was dressed in mere rags, she shivered with cold and would lie flat on her stomach to drink water from ponds. She was regularly beaten for no reason at all and was eventually turned out of the house for having stolen thirty sous, a theft of which she was quite innocent. She was taken on at another farm, where she looked after the poultry and, because she was well liked by her employers, her friends were jealous of her.

One evening in August (she was eighteen at the time), she was taken to the village fête at Colleville. She was instantly overcome, bewildered by the boisterous sounds of the fiddle music, the lamps in the trees, the array of brightly coloured clothes, the gold crosses and the lace, all those people moving as one in time to the tune. She was standing on her own, shyly, when a young man, fairly well off to judge by his appearance and who had been leaning against the shaft of a farm wagon smoking his pipe, approached her and asked her to dance. He bought her a glass of cider, a cup of coffee, a cake and a silk scarf and, imagining that she understood his motive, offered to accompany her back home. As they were walking along the edge of a field of oats, he thrust her to the ground. She was terrified and began to scream. He ran off.

One evening a little later, she was walking along the road leading to Beaumont and was trying to get past a large hay wagon as it lumbered slowly along. As she was edging her way round the wheels, she recognized Théodore.

He looked at her quite unabashed and said she should forgive his behaviour of the other night; he 'had just had too much to drink'.

She did not know how to answer him and wanted to run away.

He immediately began to talk about the harvest and various important people in the district and told her that his father had left Colleville and bought a farm at Les Ecots, which meant that they were now neighbours. 'Oh, are we!' she said. He said that his parents wanted him to settle down but that he was in no rush and preferred to wait until the right woman came along before he married. She lowered her eyes. He then asked her if she was thinking of marrying. She smiled and said that he was wrong to tease her. 'But I am not teasing you, I swear,' he said, and slipped his left arm around her waist. She walked on with his arm still around her. They were now walking more slowly. There was a gentle breeze, the stars were shining, the huge wagon-load of hay swayed from side to side in front of them and dust rose from the feet of the four horses as they plodded along. Then, without any word of command, the horses turned off to the right. He kissed her once more and she vanished into the darkness.

The following week, Théodore persuaded her to go out with him on several other occasions.

They would meet in a corner of some farmyard, behind a wall or beneath a solitary tree. Félicité was not naive like other young girls of her age; working with the farm animals had taught her a great deal. However, her natural discretion and an intuitive sense of honour prevented her from giving in to Théodore's demands. Théodore found this resistance so frustrating that, in order to satisfy his passion (or maybe out of sheer simple-mindedness), he proposed to her. She was not sure whether to believe him or not, but he insisted that he was serious.

He then announced something rather disturbing: a year ago his parents had paid for someone else to do his military service but he might still be called up at any time. The prospect of serving in the army terrified him. Félicité took this cowardice as a sign of his affection for her and it made her love him all the more. She would slip out of the house at night to meet Théodore, who assailed her with his fears and entreaties.

Eventually, he declared that he would go to the Préfecture himself and find out what the situation was. He would come back and tell Félicité the following Sunday, between eleven o'clock and midnight.

At the appointed time, Félicité ran to meet her lover.

But instead of Théodore, it was one of his friends who stood waiting to meet her.

He informed her that she would never see Théodore again. In order to make sure he could not be called up, he had married a wealthy old lady from Toucques, by the name of Madame Lehoussais.

Félicité's distress was unbounded. She threw herself to the ground, weeping and wailing; she implored God to come to her aid and lay moaning, all alone in the fields, until daylight. Then she made her way back to the farm and announced that she had decided to leave. At the end of the month, having received her wages, she wrapped her few belongings in a shawl and left for Pont-l'Evêque.

Outside the inn she spoke to a woman wearing a widow's hood who, as it happened, was looking for a cook. The young girl knew precious little about cooking but she seemed so willing and so ready to oblige that Madame Aubain eventually said: 'Very well, you may work for me.'

A quarter of an hour later, Félicité was installed in her house.

At first she lived in a constant state of trepidation as a result of 'the sort of house it was' and the memory of 'Monsieur' which seemed to hover over everything! Paul and Virginie, one aged seven and the other barely four, seemed made of some precious material; she liked to give them piggyback rides and was mortified when Madame Aubain instructed her not to keep kissing them. Even so, she was happy. Her new surroundings were very pleasant and her earlier unhappiness quickly faded.

Every Thursday, a group of Madame Aubain's friends came to play Boston. Félicité would set out the cards and the foot-warmers in readiness. The guests always arrived punctually at eight and left as the clock struck eleven.

On Monday mornings, the secondhand dealer who had a shop at the end of the lane would spread his various bits and pieces of ironmongery out on the pavement. The town would be filled with the buzz of voices, with the sounds of horses neighing, lambs bleating, pigs grunting and carts rattling through the streets. At about midday, just when the market was at its busiest, an old peasant would present himself on Madame Aubain's front doorstep – a tall man with a hooked nose and with his hat perched on the back of his head. This was Robelin, the farmer from Geffosses. He would be followed shortly afterwards by Liébard, the farmer from Toucques, short, fat and red in the face, wearing a grey jacket and leather gaiters complete with spurs.

They would both come bearing chickens or cheeses which they hoped they might persuade their landlady to buy. But Félicité was more than a match for their banter and they always respected her for this.

Madame Aubain also received sporadic visits from the Marquis de Grémanville, an uncle of hers who had squandered his money in loose living and who now lived at Falaise on the last bit of property he could still call his own. He would always turn up at lunch time with a loathsome little poodle which left its muddy paw marks all over the furniture. Despite his efforts to behave like a gentleman, raising his hat every time he mentioned his 'late father', habit would soon get the better of him and he would pour himself glass after glass and start telling bawdy jokes. Félicité would politely show him to the door. 'I think you have had enough for today, Monsieur de Grémanville! Do come and see us again soon!' And she would close the door behind him.

But she was always delighted to welcome Monsieur Bourais, a retired solicitor. His white cravat and bald head, the flounces on his shirt-front and the generous cut of his brown frock-coat, the special way he had of bending his arm when taking snuff, indeed everything about his person prompted in Félicité the sort of agitation we always feel when in the presence of some great man.

He looked after the management of 'Madame's' properties and would shut himself away with her for hours on end in 'Monsieur's' study. He lived in constant fear for his own reputation, had an inordinate respect for the judiciary and claimed to know some Latin.

Thinking that it would help the children to derive some enjoyment from their studies, he bought them an illustrated geography book. It depicted scenes from different parts of the world, cannibals wearing feathered head-dresses, a monkey abducting a young girl, a group of Bedouins in the desert, a whale being harpooned, and so on.

Paul carefully explained all these pictures to Félicité.

In fact, this was the only time anyone ever taught her how to read a book.

The children received their lessons from Guyot, a rather pitiful character who worked at the Town Hall, who was noted for his fine handwriting and who used to sharpen his penknife on the sole of his shoe.

Whenever the weather was fine, the whole family would get up early and spend the day at the farm at Geffosses.

The farmyard there was on a slope, with the farmhouse in the middle. One could just see the sea, a little streak of grey in the distance.

Félicité would take a few slices of cold meat from her basket and they would eat in a room adjoining the dairy. This room was all that now remained of a country house which had fallen into ruin. The paper hung in strips from the wall and fluttered in the draught. Madame Aubain sat with her head bowed, absorbed in her memories, the children hardly daring to speak. 'Off you go and play,' she would say. And off they went.

Paul would climb up into the barn, catch birds, play ducks and drakes on the pond or bang the great farm barrels with a stick to make them boom like drums.

Virginie would go and feed the rabbits or run off across the fields gathering cornflowers, showing her dainty embroidered knickers as she ran.

One evening in autumn, they were coming back through the fields.

The moon, which was in its first quarter, lit up part of the sky, and a mist drifted like a scarf over the windings of the river Toucques. A group of cattle, lying in the middle of a field, lazily watched them go by. When they came to the third field, a few of them got to their feet and stood in a circle in front of them. 'There's nothing to be frightened of!' said Félicité and, humming a wistful little tune as she approached, she went up to the nearest of the animals and patted it on the back. It turned away and the others did the same. But no sooner had they got through the next field when they heard a terrifying bellowing. It was a bull that had been hidden by the mist. It began to come towards the two women. Madame Aubain wanted to run. 'No, no, we must not move too quickly!' said Félicité. They walked more quickly, even so, and could hear the bull's loud breathing getting nearer behind them and the pounding of its hoofs on the grass. They knew it was now galloping towards them! Félicité turned round to face it, grabbed clods of earth from the ground and flung them into the bull's face. It lowered its muzzle, shook its horns and began to shudder and bellow with rage. Madame Aubain had now reached the edge of the field with the two children and was frantically trying to find a way of getting over the hedge. Félicité was still steadily retreating before the bull, throwing lumps of turf into its eyes and calling out, 'Hurry up! Hurry up!'

Madame Aubain got down into the ditch, pushing first Virginie and then Paul in front of her. She fell several times as she tried to climb the bank and at last, by dint of sheer determination, she succeeded.

The bull had driven Félicité up against a gate and was blowing slaver into her face. A second later and it would have gored her. In the nick of time she managed to squeeze herself between two bars in the gate. The huge animal was taken completely by surprise and stopped in its tracks.

People in Pont-l'Evêque talked about this adventure for years afterwards. But Félicité never boasted about it and hardly seemed to realize that she had done anything heroic.

Virginie commanded all her attention. The frightening experience with the bull had affected her nerves and Monsieur Poupart, the doctor, recommended sea bathing at Trouville.

In those days, very few people visited the resort. Madame Aubain made enquiries, sought the advice of Bourais and made preparations as if for a long journey.

The day before they left, the luggage was sent off in Liébard's farm wagon. The next day he returned with two horses. One of them had a woman's saddle with a velvet backrest and the other had a cloak rolled up across its back as a makeshift seat. Madame Aubain sat on this behind Liébard. Félicité looked after Virginie on the other horse and Paul rode separately on Monsieur Lechaptois's donkey, which had been lent on the clear understanding that they took great care of it.

The road was so bad that the five-mile journey took them two hours. The horses sank up to their pasterns in the mud and lurched forward in order to pull themselves free. They lost their footing in the ruts and sometimes had to jump. At certain points on the road, Liébard's mare would suddenly stop dead. Liébard would wait patiently for her to move forward again. As they rode on, he would tell them stories about the people who lived along the way, always adding a few personal comments of his own for good measure. In the town centre of Toucques, for instance, as they were passing alongside a house with nasturtiums growing around the windows, he said, with a shrug of his shoulders, 'There's a Madame Lehoussais lives there and, rather than take a young man . . .' Félicité did not hear the rest, for the horses had broken into a trot and the donkey had run on ahead. They turned down a track, a gate swung open, two young farmhands appeared and they all dismounted beside the manure-heap right outside the front door of the farmhouse.

Old Madame Liébard greeted her mistress with effusive expressions of delight. For lunch she served a sirloin of beef, along with tripe, black pudding, a fricassee of chicken, sparkling cider, a fruit tart and plums in brandy, all accompanied by a stream of compliments to Madame who seemed 'in much better health', to Mademoiselle who had grown up into such 'a fine looking young woman', to Monsieur Paul who was such a 'strapping' young man, not forgetting their dear departed grandparents whom the Liébards had known personally, having been in service to the family for several generations. The farm, like the Liébards themselves, had an old-world feel to it. The beams in the ceiling were pitted with woodworm, the walls blackened with smoke, the window panes grey with dust. There was an oak dresser, cluttered with all manner of implements – jugs, plates, pewter bowls, wolf-traps, shears for the sheep and a huge syringe which particularly amused the children. In the three yards outside, there was not a single tree which did not have mushrooms growing at its foot or clumps of mistletoe in its branches. Several had been blown down by the wind but had begun to grow again where the trunk had been split and all of them were bent beneath the weight of apples. The thatched roofs looked like brown velvet of unequal thickness and weathered the fiercest winds. But the shed for the carts was falling down. Madame Aubain said that she would arrange to have it repaired and asked for the horses to be reharnessed.

It took them another half-hour to reach Trouville. The little caravan had to dismount when they came to the Ecores, a cliff which jutted out over the boats below. Three minutes later they had arrived at the end of the quay and turned into the courtyard of the Golden Lamb, an inn run by old Madame David.

Virginie very quickly began to recover her strength as a result of the change of air and of bathing in the sea. She did not have a bathing costume and so she went into the water wearing a chemise. Afterwards, her maid would help her to get dressed in a customs officer's hut that was also used by the bathers.

In the afternoon, they would take the donkey and walk out beyond the Roches-Noires, towards Hennequeville. At first the path wound up between gently rolling meadows like the lawn in a park and then came to a plateau where there were grazing pastures and ploughed fields. The path was lined by holly bushes which grew amongst the tangles of brambles, and here and there the branches of a large dead tree traced their zigzag patterns against the blue of the sky.

There was one particular field in which they usually stopped to rest themselves, looking down towards Deauville to their left, Le Havre to their right and, in front of them, the open sea. It lay shimmering in the sunshine, as smooth as the surface of a mirror and so calm that they could barely hear the murmur of the waves. Sparrows twittered from somewhere nearby and the great dome of the sky lay spread out above them. Madame Aubain would sit with her needlework, Virginie would sit beside her, plaiting rushes, Félicité gathered bunches of wild lavender and Paul, utterly bored, would always be itching to move on.

At other times they would take the ferry across the Toucques and go looking for shells. At low tide, sea urchins, ormers and jellyfish were left behind on the sand. The children would chase after flecks of foam blown about by the breeze. The waves broke lazily on the sand from one end of the beach to the other. The beach stretched as far as the eye could see but was bounded on the landward side by sand dunes which separated it from the Marais, a broad meadow in the shape of a racecourse. As they walked back through it towards Trouville, which lay at the foot of the hill, the town appeared to grow bigger at every step they took and, with its motley assortment of houses, it seemed to blossom like a flower garden in colourful disarray.

When it was too hot, they kept to their room. The dazzling brightness outside cast bars of light through the slats in the window blinds. There was not a sound to be heard in the village. Not a soul ventured out into the streets. The prevailing quiet made everything seem all the more peaceful. From far away came the sound of the caulkers' hammers beating against the hull of a boat and the smell of tar was wafted to them on the listless breeze.

The most exciting event of the day was when the fishing boats came in. Once past the entrance buoys, they would begin to tack from side to side. Their main sails would be lowered to half-mast and, with their foresail swollen like a great balloon, they would come gliding through the splashing waves right into the middle of the harbour and suddenly drop anchor. The boat would then be brought alongside the quay. The sailors would hoist their fish ashore, still live and quivering. A line of carts was ready waiting and women in cotton bonnets rushed forward to take the baskets and to kiss their menfolk.

One day one of these women came up to Félicité. A moment or two later, Félicité was back in the room at the inn, beside herself with excitement. She had found one of her lost sisters, and into the room walked Nastasie Barette, now Leroux, with a baby at her breast, another child holding her right hand and, on her left, a little ship's boy with his hands on his hips and his beret over one ear.

After a quarter of an hour, Madame Aubain asked her to leave.

But after that there was no getting away from them. They would wait just outside the kitchen or follow them when they went for walks. The husband always kept well out of sight.

Félicité became very attached to them. She bought them a blanket, some shirts and a cooking stove. They were obviously out to take advantage of her. Madame Aubain was annoyed that Félicité was not more firm with them. She also took objection to the familiar way in which the nephew spoke to Paul. So, because Virginie had developed a cough and the weather had taken a turn for the worse, she returned to Pont-l'Evêque.

Monsieur Bourais offered his advice on choosing a good school for Paul. The one at Caen was generally considered to be the best. So Paul was sent away to Caen. He said his goodbyes bravely, really quite pleased that he was going to live somewhere where he would have some friends of his own.

Madame Aubain resigned herself to her son going away, knowing that he must have a good education. Virginie quickly got used to being on her own, but Félicité

17

found the house very quiet without him. Soon, however, she had something else to occupy her mind. From Christmas onwards she had to take Virginie to catechism every day.

3

Genuflecting as she went in through the door, Félicité walked up the aisle beneath the high ceiling of the nave, opened the door of Madame Aubain's pew, sat herself down and looked all around her.

The children were seated in the choir stalls, the boys on the right and the girls on the left. The priest stood in front of them beside the lectern. One of the stained-glass windows in the apse showed the Holy Spirit looking down on the Virgin Mary. In another, the Virgin knelt before the infant Jesus and behind the tabernacle there was a carving in wood representing Saint Michael slaying the dragon.

The priest began with a summary of the Holy Scriptures. Félicité's mind was filled with images of Paradise, the Flood, the Tower of Babel, cities consumed by flames, peoples dying and idols cast down. This dazzling recital of events instilled in her a wholesome respect for the Almighty and a profound fear of his wrath. She wept at the story of Christ's Passion. Why had they crucified a man who was so kind to children, fed the hungry, gave sight to the blind, and who had chosen, out of his own gentle nature, to be born amongst the poor on the rough straw of a stable? Seed-time and harvest, the fruits of the vine, all those familiar things mentioned in the gospels had their place in her life too. They now seemed sanctified by contact with God. Félicité loved lambs all the more because of her love for the Lamb of God, and doves now reminded her of the Holy Spirit.

She found it difficult to imagine what the Holy Spirit actually looked like because he was not only a bird but sometimes a fire and sometimes a breath. Perhaps it was the light of the Holy Spirit that she would see at night-time, flickering at the edge of the marshes, or his breath which drove the clouds across the sky, or his voice which made the church bells ring so beautifully. She sat rapt in adoration of these wonders, delighting in the coolness of the stone walls and the peacefulness of the church.

Of church dogma she understood not a word and did not even attempt to understand it. As the curé stood explaining it all to the children and the children repeated what they had learnt, Félicité would drop off to sleep, to be woken suddenly by the clatter of wooden shoes on the stone floor as the children left the church. And so Félicité came to learn her catechism by dint of hearing the children recite it, for her own religious education had been neglected when she was young. From then on, she copied the religious observances of Virginie, fasting when she fasted and going to confession whenever she did. For the feast of Corpus Christi, Félicité and Virginie made an altar of repose together.

For days beforehand, Félicité fretted over the preparations for Virginie's first communion. She worried about her shoes, her rosary, her missal and her gloves. Her hands trembled as she helped Madame Aubain to dress her.

All through the mass she was on tenterhooks. One half of the choir stalls was hidden from her sight by Monsieur Bourais, but straight in front of her she could see the flock of young girls all wearing white crowns over their lowered veils and looking like a field of snow. Even from a distance, she could recognize her beloved little Virginie by the delicate line of her neck and her attitude of reverent contemplation. The bell tinkled. They all bowed their heads and knelt in silence. Then, with a mighty flourish from the organ, the choir and congregation sang the *Agnus Dei*. After the boys had processed forwards, the girls stood up. With their hands joined in prayer, they moved slowly towards the candle-lit altar, knelt at the altar-step, received the Host one by one and returned in the same order to their place in the choir stalls. When it came to Virginie's turn, Félicité leant further forwards so that she could see her and, with that singular imagination that is born of true love, she felt she was herself Virginie, assuming her expression, wearing her dress and with her heart beating inside her breast. As Virginie opened her mouth, Félicité closed her eyes and almost fainted.

The next morning, bright and early, Félicité went to the sacristy and asked to be given communion. She received it with due reverence but did not experience the same rapture.

Madame Aubain wanted the best possible education for her daughter and, because Guyot was unable to teach her either English or music, she resolved to send her to the Ursuline convent school in Honfleur.

Virginie had no objection to this plan but Félicité was most unhappy and felt that Madame was being too strict. However, she came to accept that it was not really for her to decide and that her mistress probably knew best.

Then one day, an old carriage drew up outside the door. Out of it got a nun who had come to collect Mademoiselle. Félicité loaded the luggage up on to the rack, issued some parting instructions to the driver and put six pots of jam, a dozen pears and a bunch of violets in the boot.

Just as they were about to leave, Virginie burst into tears. She clung to her mother, who kissed her on the forehead and kept telling her: 'Come, come, we must be brave!' The step was pulled up and the carriage drove away.

When it had gone, Madame Aubain broke down and that evening all her friends, Monsieur and Madame Lormeau, Madame Lechaptois, the two Rochefeuille sisters, Monsieur de Houppeville and Bourais, came round to comfort her.

At first, the loss of her daughter left her feeling very sad. But she received letters from her on three days each week and on the other days she wrote back to her, walked in her garden, read a little and so managed to occupy her time.

Every morning, out of habit, Félicité would go into Virginie's bedroom and gaze at the walls. She missed being able to comb her hair for her, tie her bootlaces and tuck her up in bed; she missed seeing her sweet little face always beside her and holding her hand when they went out for walks. For want of something to do, she tried to take up lace work. But she was too clumsy with her fingers and she kept breaking the threads. She could not put her mind to anything and was losing sleep. She was, in her own words, 'all empty inside'.

In order to provide herself with 'a bit of company', she asked Madame Aubain if her nephew Victor might be allowed to visit her.

He would always arrive on Sundays, just after mass, rosy-cheeked, his shirt unbuttoned and bringing with him the smells of the countryside through which he had travelled. She straight away laid the table for him. They would eat lunch sitting opposite each other, Félicité taking care to eat as little as possible so as to save on expense and giving Victor so much to eat that he ended up falling asleep. As the first bell for vespers began to ring, she would wake him up, give his trousers a good brush, tie his tie, and make her way to church, leaning on his arm like a proud mother.

His parents always told him to make sure he brought something back with him, a bag of sugar, a piece of soap, a little brandy or even money. He brought with him any of his clothes that needed mending and Félicité always did the work willingly, glad of any opportunity of encouraging him to visit her again.

In August, Victor went to join his father on his sea trips along the coast.

It was the beginning of the school holidays and it was some consolation to Félicité to have the children back at home. But Paul had become rather temperamental and Virginie was now too grown-up to be treated as a little child, which created a sense of awkwardness and distance between them.

Victor's travels took him to Morlaix, to Dunkirk and to Brighton and after each trip he brought back a present for Félicité. The first was a little box made out of shells, the second a coffee cup and the third a big gingerbread man. He was growing into a handsome young man, with a fine figure, the first signs of a moustache, a frank and open expression and a little leather cap which he wore perched on the back of his head like a sea pilot. He would entertain Félicité by telling her stories laced with all sorts of nautical jargon.

One Monday, 14 July 1819 (it was a date that Félicité was never to forget), Victor announced that he had been signed on to the crew of an ocean-going ship and that in two days' time he would be taking the night ferry from Honfleur to join his schooner, which was due shortly to set sail from Le Havre. He might be away for two years.

The prospect of such a long separation left Félicité

feeling very saddened. In order to say one final farewell to him, on the Wednesday evening, after Madame had finished her dinner, she put on her clogs and ran the ten miles from Pont-l'Evêque to Honfleur.

When she came to the Calvary, instead of turning left, she turned right, got lost in the shipyards and had to retrace her steps. She asked directions from some passers-by, who told her she would have to hurry. She walked all the way round the harbour, which was full of boats, getting caught up in the moorings as she went. Suddenly the ground seemed to fall away beneath her, beams of light criss-crossed before her eyes and she thought she must be losing her senses when she saw some horses in the sky overhead.

On the quayside, more horses were neighing, frightened by the sea. They were being hoisted into the air by a derrick and then lowered into a boat which was already crammed with passengers trying to squeeze their way between barrels of cider, baskets of cheese and sacks of grain. Hens were cackling and the captain was swearing. One of the deck-hands, apparently oblivious to everything around him, stood leaning against the cat-head. Félicité had not recognized him and was calling out 'Victor!' again and again. He looked up and she rushed forward, but just at that moment the gangway was suddenly pulled ashore.

The boat moved out of the harbour, hauled along by a group of women who sang in chorus as they went about their work. Its ribs creaked and heavy waves lashed its bows. The sail swung round and hid everyone from view. The surface of the sea shone like silver in the moonlight and on it the ship appeared as a black spot, growing paler as it moved away. Eventually it was swallowed up in the distance and vanished from sight.

Returning home, Félicité passed by the Calvary and was taken by a sudden desire to commend to God's mercy all that she held dear. She stood there praying for a long time, with tears running down her cheeks and her eyes fixed on the clouds above. The town was fast asleep; the only people about were the customs men. Water could be heard gushing through the holes in the lock-gate like a running torrent. A clock struck two.

The convent would not be open to visitors before daybreak and Félicité knew that, if she arrived back late, Madame was sure to be annoyed. So, although she would have loved just one small kiss from Virginie, she set off back home. The maids at the inn were just waking up as she walked into Pont-l'Evêque.

So poor little Victor was to spend months on end being tossed around on the waves! His previous trips at sea had not bothered her. England and Brittany were places one came back from. But America, the colonies and the Antilles were lost in some unknown region on the other side of the world.

From the day he left, Félicité could not stop thinking about her nephew. When it was hot and sunny, she worried that he might be thirsty and when there was a storm, she feared he might be struck by lightning. As she listened to the wind howling in the chimney and blowing slates off the roof, she pictured him buffeted by the same storm, clinging to the top of a broken mast and being flung backwards into a sheet of foam. At other times, prompted by her recollection of the pictures in the geography book, she imagined him being eaten by savages, captured by monkeys in a forest or dying on some deserted beach. But she never spoke about these worries to anyone.

Madame Aubain had worries of her own about her daughter.

The sisters at the convent said that she was an affectionate child, but over-sensitive. The slightest emotion unsettled her and she had to give up playing the piano.

Her mother insisted that she wrote home regularly. One morning, when the postman had failed to appear, she could scarcely contain her impatience and kept pacing backwards and forwards in her room between her armchair and the window. This really was extraordinary! No news for four days!

Thinking that her own situation might serve as some comfort to her mistress, Félicité ventured:

'But Madame, I haven't received any news for six months!'

'News from whom?'

'Why, news from my nephew,' Félicité gently replied.

'Oh, your nephew!' And with a shrug of her shoulders, Madame Aubain began pacing about the room again, as if to say, 'I hadn't given him a thought! And in any case, he's no concern of mine! A mere ship's boy, a scrounger; he's not worth bothering about! But someone like my daughter . . . Really!'

Although Félicité had been fed such rough treatment since she was a child, she felt very offended by Madame Aubain. But she soon got over it.

After all, it was to be expected that Madame should get upset about her own daughter.

For Félicité, the two children were of equal importance; they were bound together by her love for them and it seemed right that they should share the same fate.

Félicité learnt from the chemist that Victor's ship had arrived in Havana. He had read the announcement in a newspaper.

Because of its association with cigars, Félicité imagined Havana to be a place in which the only thing people did was to smoke and she pictured Victor walking amongst crowds of Negroes in a cloud of tobacco smoke. Was it possible to return from Havana by land, 'if need be'? How far was it from Pont-l'Evêque? In order to find out, she went to consult Monsieur Bourais.

He reached for his atlas and launched into a disquisition on lines of longitude. Félicité was utterly bewildered. Bourais sat in front of her, beaming smugly to himself, like the know-all he was. Eventually, he picked up his pencil and pointed to an almost invisible black dot in one of the little indentations in the contour of an oval-shaped patch on the map. 'Here it is,' he said. Félicité peered closely at the map. The network of coloured lines was a strain on her eyes, but it told her nothing. Bourais asked her what was puzzling her and she asked him if he would show her the house in which Victor was living. Bourais raised his arms in the air, sneezed and roared with laughter, delighted to come across someone so simple-minded. Félicité, whose understanding was so limited that she probably even expected to see a picture of her nephew, could not understand what he found so funny.

It was a fortnight after this, at his usual time on market day, that Liébard came into the kitchen and handed Félicité a letter which he had received from her brother-in-law. As neither of them could read, Félicité showed the letter to her mistress.

Madame Aubain, who was counting the stitches on a piece of knitting, put her work to one side, opened the letter, gave a sudden start and then, lowering her voice and looking very serious, she said, 'They are sending you . . . bad news. Your nephew . . .'

Victor was dead. That was all the letter said.

Félicité sank down on to a chair and leant her head against the wall. Her eyelids closed and suddenly flushed pink. She remained there, her head bowed, her hands hanging limply at her side, staring in front of her and repeating over and over again, 'The poor boy! The poor boy!'

Liébard stood looking at her and sighing. Madame Aubain was shaking slightly.

She suggested that Félicité might go and see her sister at Trouville.

Félicité gave a wave of her hand to indicate that it was not necessary.

There was a silence. Old Liébard thought it best to leave.

When he had gone, Félicité said, 'It doesn't matter a bit, not to them it doesn't.'

She lowered her head again and sat there, now and then toying distractedly with the knitting needles that lay on the work-table.

A group of women passed by in the yard, wheeling a barrow-load of dripping linen.

Félicité caught sight of them through the window and suddenly remembered that she had washing to do herself. She had passed the lye through it the day before and today it needed rinsing. She got up and left the room.

Her washing board and her tub were on the bank of the Toucques. She flung her pile of chemises on to the ground beside the river, rolled up her sleeves and seized her battledore. The drubbing could be heard in all the neighbouring gardens. The fields lay deserted and the wind rippled the surface of the river. On the river-bed, long strands of weed drifted with the current, like the hair of corpses floating downstream in the water. Félicité managed to restrain her grief and was very brave until the evening, but when she was alone in her room she gave in to it, lying prone on her mattress with her face buried in the pillow and pressing her fists to her temples.

Much later, she came to learn the circumstances of Victor's death from the captain of his ship. He had caught yellow fever and had been bled too much in the hospital. Four separate doctors had given him the same treatment and he had died immediately. The chief doctor's comment was, 'Good, that's one more to add to the list!'

Victor had always been treated cruelly by his parents and Félicité preferred not to see them again. They did not get in touch with Félicité either; perhaps they had simply forgotten about her or perhaps poverty had hardened their hearts.

Virginie was now growing weaker.

Difficulty in breathing, a persistent cough, a constant high temperature and pale blotches on her cheeks all pointed to some underlying disorder. Monsieur Poupart had advised a holiday in Provence. Madame Aubain decided to follow his advice and would have brought Virginie back home immediately, had it not been for the weather at Pont-l'Evêque.

She had a standing arrangement with a job-master, who drove her to the convent every Tuesday. In the convent garden there was a terrace overlooking the Seine where Virginie would walk up and down over the fallen vine leaves, leaning on her mother's arm. She would look out at the sails in the distance and the whole sweep of the estuary from the chateau at Tancarville to the lighthouses at Le Havre. Sometimes the sun would suddenly break through the clouds and make her blink. Afterwards, they would rest under the arbour. Her mother had procured a little flask of the choicest Malaga wine, from which Virginie would take just two tiny sips, laughing at the thought of making herself tipsy.

She began to recover her strength. Autumn gradually slipped by. Félicité did all she could to reassure Madame Aubain. But one evening, on her way back from an errand in the town, she noticed Monsieur Poupart's gig standing at the front door. Monsieur Poupart himself was in the entrance hall and Madame Aubain was fastening her bonnet.

'Bring me my foot-warmer, my purse and my gloves! Hurry!'

Virginie had pneumonia and Madame feared she was beyond recovery.

'I'm sure it's not that bad,' said the doctor, and the two of them climbed into his carriage, with the snowflakes falling in great flurries around them. Night was drawing on and it was bitterly cold.

Félicité dashed into the church to light a candle and then began to run after Monsieur Poupart's gig. It was a full hour before she caught up with it. She jumped up behind it and clung to the fringe. Suddenly a thought occurred to her. 'The gate to the courtyard was not locked! What if thieves should break in!' She jumped back down on to the road.

The next day, at the very first sign of daylight, she went to the doctor's house. The doctor had returned but had already left again to visit patients in the country. She waited at the inn, thinking that someone or other might arrive with a letter. Eventually, in the half-light of morning, she boarded the Lisieux stagecoach.

The convent was situated at the foot of a steep narrow street. When she was about half-way down the street, she began to make out strange sounds coming from the convent; it was the tolling of a death bell. 'It must be for someone else', she thought, and gave the door-knocker a loud rap.

After some considerable time, she heard the shuffle of footsteps, the door was inched open and a nun appeared.

The good sister solemnly announced that 'she had just passed away'. At precisely the same moment, the bell of Saint-Léonard's began to toll even more strongly.

Félicité went up to the second floor.

She stood in the doorway of the bedroom and could see Virginie laid out on her back, her hands clasped together, her mouth open and her head tilted backwards. Above her head and inclined towards her was a black crucifix; her face was whiter than the drapes which hung stiffly around her. Madame Aubain lay hugging the foot of the bed and sobbing wildly. The Mother Superior stood beside her on the right. On the chest of drawers, three candlesticks gave out little circles of red light; outside, the fog whitened the window panes. Some nuns came and led Madame Aubain away.

Félicité did not leave Virginie's bedside for two whole

nights. She sat there, repeating the same prayers over and over again; she would get up to sprinkle holy water on the sheets, then come back to her chair and continue to gaze fixedly at the dead girl. At the end of her first night's vigil, she noticed that her face was beginning to turn yellow, her lips were turning blue, her nose had grown thinner and her eyes had become sunken. More than once she kissed her eyes and would not have been in the least surprised if Virginie had opened them again; to minds like hers, the supernatural appears perfectly ordinary. She laid her out, wrapped her in her shroud, put her in her coffin, placed a wreath upon her and spread out her hair. Her hair was fair and amazingly long for a girl of her age. Félicité cut off a large lock of it and slipped half of it into her bosom, resolving that it would never be separated from her.

The body was brought back to Pont-l'Evêque, according to Madame Aubain's instructions. Madame Aubain followed the hearse in a closed carriage.

After the funeral mass, it took another three-quarters of an hour to get to the cemetery. Paul led the procession, sobbing. Monsieur Bourais walked behind him, followed in turn by various dignitaries from Pont-l'Evêque, the women, all wearing black veils, and lastly Félicité. Félicité could not help thinking of her nephew and, having been unable to offer him these last honours, she now felt an added grief, as if he were being buried along with Virginie.

Madame Aubain's despair knew no bounds.

At first she rebelled against God, thinking it was unjust

that He should take her daughter from her when she had never done any wrong and when there was nothing for her to feel guilty about. But perhaps there was. She should have taken her to the South. Other doctors would have cured her. She blamed herself, wished she could follow her daughter to the grave and called out in anguish in the middle of her dreams. One dream in particular tormented her. Her husband, dressed like a sailor, had returned from a long voyage and, choking back his tears, told her that he had received an order to take Virginie away. They then both racked their brains to think of a hiding place for her.

On one occasion she came in from the garden distraught. Just a moment before (and she pointed to the spot), the father and daughter had appeared in front of her, one after the other. They were not doing anything; they were just staring at her.

For several months she remained in her room, totally listless. Félicité gently admonished her, telling her that she should look after herself for the sake of her son and her late husband and in memory of 'her'.

'Her?' said Madame Aubain as though waking from sleep. 'Oh yes, of course. You haven't forgotten her, have you!' This was a reference to the cemetery, which Madame Aubain had been expressly forbidden to visit.

Félicité went there every day.

On the stroke of four, she would walk past the row of houses, climb the hill, open the gate and approach

Virginie's grave. There was a little column of pink marble standing on a stone base, with a small garden surrounded by chains. The separate beds could hardly be seen beneath the covering of flowers. Félicité would water the leaves, place fresh sand on the garden and get down on her hands and knees to make sure the ground was properly weeded. When Madame Aubain was eventually able to come to see the grave, she found it a source of comfort, a kind of consolation for her loss.

The years passed, one very much like another, marked only by the annual recurrence of the church festivals: Easter, the Assumption, All Saints' Day. It was only little incidents in their daily lives that, in later years, enabled them to recall a particular date. Thus in 1825 two glaziers whitewashed the entrance hall; in 1827 a part of the roof fell into the courtyard and nearly killed a passer-by. In the summer of 1828 it was Madame's turn to distribute consecrated bread to the parishioners. This was also about the same time that Bourais mysteriously left the town. One by one, all their old acquaintances went away: Guyot, Liébard, Madame Lechaptois, Robelin and old Uncle Gremanville, who had been paralysed for many years.

One night, the driver of the mail-coach arrived in Pont-l'Evêque with news of the July Revolution. A few days later, a new subprefect was appointed: the Baron de Larsonnière, who had previously been a consul in America. He arrived in Pont-l'Evêque accompanied not only by his wife but also by his sister-in-law and three young girls, all of them already quite grown up. They were often to be seen on their lawn, dressed in long, flowing smocks. They also had a Negro servant and a parrot. They called on Madame Aubain to pay their respects and she made a point of doing likewise. As soon as she spotted them approaching in the distance, Félicité would come running in to tell Madame Aubain that they were on their way. But there was only one thing that could really awaken her interest and that was her son's letters.

Paul seemed unable to settle down to a career and spent much of his time in the tavern. Madame Aubain would pay off his debts, but he immediately ran up new ones. She would sit at her knitting by the window and heave sighs that Félicité could hear even in the kitchen, where she was working at her spinning wheel.

The two women would often take a stroll together alongside the trellised wall of the garden. They still talked constantly about Virginie, wondering whether she would have liked such and such a thing or trying to imagine what she would have said on such and such an occasion.

All her belongings were still in a cupboard in the children's bedroom. Madame Aubain had avoided looking inside it as much as possible. Then, one summer day, she resigned herself. Moths came flying from the cupboard.

Virginie's frocks hung in a row beneath a shelf upon which there were three dolls, some hoops, a set of doll's furniture and her own hand-basin. The two women took out all the petticoats, stockings and handkerchiefs and spread them out on the two beds before folding them again. This sorry collection of objects lay there, caught in a beam of sunlight which brought out all the stains and the creases that had been made by the movements of Virginie's body. The air was warm, the sky was blue, a blackbird sang outside and the world seemed to be utterly at peace. They found a little chestnut-coloured hat made of long-piled plush, but it had been completely destroyed by the moths. Félicité asked if she might have it as a keepsake. The two women looked at each other and their eyes filled with tears. Madame Aubain opened her arms and Félicité threw herself into them. Mistress and servant embraced each other, uniting their grief in a kiss which made them equal.

It was the first time that this had ever happened, Madame Aubain being, by nature, very reserved. Félicité could not have been more grateful if she had been offered a priceless gift and from then on she doted on her mistress with dog-like fidelity and the reverence that might be accorded to a saint.

As time went by, Félicité's natural kind-heartedness increased.

One day she heard the sound of drums from a regiment marching along the street and she stood at the door with a jug of cider, handing out drinks to the soldiers. She helped to nurse cholera victims and to look after the refugees from Poland. One of the Poles even said he would like to marry her, but they had a serious argument when she came back one morning from the angelus to find him ensconced in her kitchen, calmly helping himself to a salad which she had prepared for lunch.

After the Poles had left, she turned her attention to an old man by the name of Colmiche, who was rumoured to have committed terrible atrocities in '93. He now lived down by the river in a ruined pigsty. The boys in the town used to spy on him through the cracks in the wall and throw stones at him as he lay coughing and choking on his straw bed. He had long, straggling hair, his eyelids were inflamed and on one arm there was a swelling bigger than his head. Félicité provided him with linen and did what she could to keep his hovel clean; she even hoped she might be able to install him in the outhouse, where he would not disturb Madame. When the tumour burst, she changed his dressing every single day. Sometimes she would bring him a small piece of cake or help him outside on to a bundle of straw, where he could lie in the sun. The poor old wretch would splutter and shake and thank her in a barely audible whisper, saying he could not bear to lose her and stretching out his hands the minute he saw her preparing to leave him. He died and Félicité had a mass said for the repose of his soul.

On the same day, she received the most wonderful surprise. Just as she was serving dinner, Madame de Larsonnière's Negro servant arrived, carrying the parrot in its cage, along with its perch, chain and padlock. There was a note from the Baroness, informing Madame Aubain that her husband had been promoted to a Préfecture and that they were leaving Pont-l'Evêque that very evening. She asked Madame Aubain if she would be kind enough to accept the parrot as a memento of their friendship and as a token of her respect.

The parrot had been a source of wonder to Félicité for a long time, for it came from America, a word which always reminded her of Victor. She had already questioned the servant about it and, on one occasion, had even said that 'Madame would be delighted to look after it!'

The Negro had mentioned this to his mistress and, because she could not take it away with her, she readily seized this opportunity of getting it off her hands.

4

The parrot was called Loulou. His body was green, the tips of his wings were pink, the top of his head was blue and his breast was gold-coloured.

Unfortunately, he had the tiresome habit of chewing his perch and he kept plucking out his feathers, scattering his droppings everywhere and splashing the water from his bath all over his cage. He thoroughly irritated Madame Aubain and so she gave him to Félicité to look after.

She decided she would teach him to speak and he was very soon able to say, 'Pretty boy!', 'Your servant, sir!' and 'Hail Mary!' She put him near the front door and a number of visitors were surprised that he would not answer to the name 'Polly', which is what all parrots are supposed to be called. Some people said he looked more like a turkey or called him a blockhead. Félicité found their jibes very hurtful. There was a curious stubborn streak in Loulou which never ceased to amaze Félicité; he would refuse to talk the minute anyone looked at him!

Even so, there was no doubt that he appreciated company. On Sundays, when the Rochefeuille sisters, Monsieur de Houppeville and some of Madame Aubain's new friends – the apothecary Onfroy, Monsieur Varin and Captain Mathieu – came round to play cards, Loulou would beat on the window panes with his wings and make such a furious commotion that no one could hear themselves speak.

He obviously found Bourais's face a source of great amusement. He only had to see it and he would break into fits of uncontrollable laughter. His squawks could be heard echoing round the yard. The neighbours would come to their windows and start laughing too. To avoid being seen by the parrot, Bourais would slink past the house along the side of the wall, hiding his face behind his hat. He would go down to the river and come into the house by way of the back garden. The looks he gave the bird were not of the tender variety.

The butcher's boy had once flipped Loulou on the ear for trying to help himself to something from his basket and, since then, Loulou always tried to give him a peck through his shirt. Fabu threatened to wring his neck, although he was not cruel by nature, despite what the tattoos on his arms and his long side whiskers might have led one to believe. In fact, he was rather fond of the parrot and, just for the fun of it, he had even tried to teach him a few swear words. Félicité was alarmed at the thought of his acquiring such bad habits and moved him into the kitchen. His chain was removed and he was allowed to wander all over the house.

When he came down the stairs, he would position the curved part of his beak on the step in front of him and then raise first his right foot, followed by his left. Félicité was always worried that these weird acrobatics would make the parrot giddy. He fell ill and could not talk or eat due to an ulcer under his tongue, such as chickens sometimes have. Félicité cured him herself, extracting the lump in his mouth with her fingernails. One day, Monsieur Paul was silly enough to blow cigar smoke up his nose. On another occasion, when Madame Lormeau was teasing him with the end of her parasol, he bit off the metal ferrule with his beak. Then there was the time he got lost.

Félicité had put him out on the grass to get some fresh air. She went indoors for a minute and, when she came back, the parrot had disappeared. She searched for him in the bushes, by the river and even on the rooftops, oblivious to her mistress's shouts of 'Do be careful! You must be mad!' She then hunted through every single garden in Pont-l'Evêque and stopped all the people in the street, asking, 'You don't happen to have seen my parrot by any chance?' Those who did not already know the parrot were given a full description. Suddenly, she thought she saw something green flying about behind the mills at the bottom of the hill. But when she got to the top of the hill, there was nothing to be seen. A pedlar told her he had definitely seen the bird only a short while ago in old Madame Simon's shop at Saint-Melaine. Félicité ran all the way there, but nobody knew what she was talking about. In the end she came back home, utterly exhausted, her shoes torn to shreds and feeling sick at heart. She sat down on the middle of the garden bench, next to Madame, and she was telling her everything that she had done when she suddenly felt something drop gently on to her shoulder. It was Loulou! What on earth had he been up to? Perhaps he had just gone for a little walk around the town!

It took Félicité quite a while to recover from this shock. If the truth were known, she never really recovered from it completely.

She caught tonsillitis, as a result of getting thoroughly chilled, and shortly afterwards developed pains in her ears. Within three years she was completely deaf and spoke in a very loud voice, even in church. Even though her sins could have been proclaimed in every corner of the diocese without bringing any discredit to her or causing offence to others, the curé decided that it would now be best to hear her confession in the sacristy.

Imaginary buzzing noises in her head added to her troubles. Her mistress would often say, 'Goodness me!

You're just being silly!' Félicité would answer, 'Yes, Madame,' still looking around her to see where the noises were coming from.

She became enclosed in an ever-diminishing world of her own; gone for ever was the pealing of church bells and the lowing of cattle in the fields. Every living thing passed by her in ghostly silence. Only one sound now reached her ears, and that was the voice of her parrot.

Almost as if he were deliberately trying to entertain her, he would imitate the clicking of the turnspit, the shrill cry of the fishmonger or the sound of sawing from the joiner's shop on the other side of the street. Whenever the front door bell rang, he would imitate Madame Aubain: 'Félicité! The door, the door!'

They would hold conversations with each other, the parrot endlessly repeating the three stock phrases from his repertory and Félicité replying with words that made very little sense but which all came straight from the heart. In her isolation, Loulou was almost a son to her; she simply doted on him. He used to climb up her fingers, peck at her lips and hang on to her shawl. Sometimes she would put her face close to his and shake her head in the way a nurse does to a baby, with the wings of her bonnet and the bird's wings all fluttering together.

When storm clouds gathered and thunder rumbled, the bird would squawk loudly, no doubt remembering the sudden cloud-bursts of his native forests. The sound of falling rain would send him into a frenzy. He would fly madly about the house, shooting up to the ceiling, knocking everything over and finally escaping through the window into the garden to splash around in the puddles. But he would soon come back, perch on one of the fire-dogs, jump up and down to dry his feathers and then proudly display his tail or his beak.

One morning in the terrible winter of 1837, when she had put him near the fireplace because of the cold, she found him dead in his cage, hanging head downwards with his claws caught in the metal bars. He had probably died of a stroke, but the thought crossed Félicité's mind that he might have been poisoned with parsley and, although there was no definite proof, her suspicions fell on Fabu.

She wept so much that her mistress eventually said, 'Well, why don't you have him stuffed?'

Félicité went to consult the chemist, who had always been kind to the parrot.

He wrote to Le Havre and a man by the name of Fellacher agreed to do the job. But, knowing that the mail-coach sometimes mislaid parcels, Félicité decided that she would take the parrot as far as Honfleur herself.

The road ran between endless lines of apple trees, bare and leafless. Ice lay in the ditches. Dogs barked as she walked past the farms. With her hands tucked under her mantlet and her basket on her arm, Félicité walked briskly along the middle of the road in her little black clogs.

She followed the road through the forest, passed Le Haut-Chêne and eventually reached Saint-Gatien.

On the road behind her, in a cloud of dust and gathering speed on its way down the hill, a mail-coach at full gallop came rushing towards her like a whirlwind. The coachman, seeing that this woman was making no attempt to get out of the way, stood up and looked out over the roof of the carriage and both he and his postilion shouted at her for all their worth. The four horses, which he was vainly trying to rein in, galloped faster and faster towards her and the leading pair struck her as they went by. With a sharp tug on the reins, the coachman forced them to swerve on to the side of the road. In his rage, he raised his arm and lashed out at her with his long whip as the coach lurched past. The blow struck Félicité full across her face and the upper part of her body, and with such force that she fell flat on her back.

The first thing she did when she regained consciousness was to open her basket. Fortunately, Loulou had come to no harm. She felt a burning sensation on her right cheek. She put her hand to her face and saw that her hand was red. She was bleeding.

She sat down on a pile of stones and dabbed her face with her handkerchief. Then she ate a crust of bread which she had brought with her in case she needed it and tried to take her mind off her wound by looking at the parrot.

As she came to the top of the hill at Ecquemauville, she saw the lights of Honfleur twinkling in the night like clusters of stars and, beyond them, the sea, stretching dimly into the distance. She was suddenly overcome with a fit of giddiness and her wretched childhood, the disappointment of her first love affair, the departure of her nephew and the death of Virginie all came flooding back to her like the waves of an incoming tide, welling up inside her and taking her breath away.

She insisted on speaking personally to the captain of the ship and, although she did not tell him what was in her parcel, she asked him to look after it carefully.

Fellacher kept the parrot for a long time. He kept promising that it would arrive the following week. After six months, he announced that a box had been dispatched, but that was the last they heard of it. Félicité began to fear that Loulou would never come back. 'He has been stolen, I know it!' she thought to herself.

But at last he arrived. And quite magnificent he looked too, perched on a branch which was screwed on to a mahogany plinth, with one foot held raised, his head cocked to one side and holding in his beak a nut which the taxidermist, in order to add a little touch of grandeur, had gilded.

Félicité installed him in her room.

This room, which few were allowed into, was filled with a mixture of religious knick-knacks and other miscellaneous bits and pieces and resembled something between a chapel and a bazaar.

A large wardrobe made it awkward to open the door fully. Opposite the window that looked out on to the garden was a smaller circular window which looked out on to the courtyard. There was a plain, unsprung bed and beside it a table with a water jug, two combs and a small cake of blue soap on a chipped plate. Fixed to the walls were rosaries, medals, several pictures of the Virgin and a holy-water stoop made out of a coconut shell. On the chest of drawers, which was draped with a cloth like an altar, was the shell box that Victor had given her, a watering can and a ball, some handwriting books, the illustrated geography book and a pair of little ankle boots. Hanging by its two ribbons from the nail which supported the mirror was the little plush hat! These keepsakes meant so much to Félicité. She had even kept one of Monsieur's frock-coats. If there was anything that Madame Aubain wanted to get rid of, she would find a place for it in her room, like the artificial flowers beside her chest of drawers and the portrait of the Comte d'Artois in the window recess.

Loulou was placed on a little shelf made especially for the purpose and fixed to a chimney breast which protruded into the room. Every morning, as she woke, she would catch sight of him in the early morning light and would recall the days gone by, trivial incidents, right down to the tiniest detail, remembered not in sadness but in perfect tranquillity.

Being unable to hold a conversation with anyone, she lived her life as if in a sleepwalker's trance. The only thing that seemed capable of bringing her back to life was the Corpus Christi procession, when she would visit all the neighbours, collecting candlesticks and mats to decorate the altar of repose that was always set up outside in the street.

When she went to church, she would sit gazing at the picture of the Holy Spirit and it struck her that it looked rather like her parrot. The resemblance was even more striking in an Epinal colour print depicting Our Lord's baptism. The dove had wings of crimson and a body of emerald-green and it looked for all the world like Loulou. Félicité bought the picture and hung it in place of the portrait of the Comte d'Artois, so that she could see them both together at the same time. In her mind, the one became associated with the other, the parrot becoming sanctified by connection with the Holy Spirit and the Holy Spirit in turn acquiring added life and meaning. Surely it could not have been a dove that God had chosen to speak through, since doves cannot talk. It must have been one of Loulou's ancestors. Félicité would say her prayers with her eyes turned towards the picture but every now and then she would turn her head slightly to look at the parrot.

She thought of entering the sisterhood of the Ladies of the Virgin but Madame Aubain persuaded her not to.

There now occurred an event of considerable importance – Paul's wedding.

Having worked first as a lawyer's clerk, Paul had subsequently tried his hand at business, worked for the Customs and for the Inland Revenue and had even considered joining the Department of Forests and Waterways. Now, at the age of thirty-six, as if by divine inspiration, he had suddenly discovered his vocation – the Registry Office! Indeed, he had displayed such a talent for the job that one of the inspectors had offered him his daughter's hand in marriage and had promised to use his influence to advance his career.

By now, Paul took his responsibilities seriously and he brought his intended to see his mother.

Not a thing at Pont-l'Evêque met with her approval. She expected to be treated like royalty and she hurt Félicité's feelings badly. Madame Aubain was relieved to see her go.

The following week, they learned of the death of Monsieur Bourais in an inn somewhere in Lower Brittany. Rumour had it that he had committed suicide. This turned out to be true and questions were raised about his honesty. Madame Aubain went through her accounts and the catalogue of his misdeeds soon became apparent: embezzlement of arrears of rent, undeclared sales of wood, forged receipts, and so forth. It was also discovered that he was the father of an illegitimate child and that he was having 'an illicit relationship with someone from Dozulé'.

This sordid business was a source of great distress to Madame Aubain. In March 1853, she began to feel pains in her chest. A grey coating covered her tongue. She was treated with leeches but this failed to improve her breathing. On the ninth evening of her illness, she died, aged just seventy-two.

People took her to be younger than this because of her dark hair, which she had always worn in bandeaux round her pale, pockmarked face. She had very few friends to lament her death; there was a certain haughtiness about her that had always kept people at a distance.

Félicité wept for her in a way that servants rarely weep for their masters. That Madame should die before her disturbed her whole way of thinking; it seemed to go against the natural order of things; it was something unacceptable and unreal.

Ten days later, just as soon as they could get there from Besançon, the heirs arrived on the scene. Madame Aubain's daughter-in-law went through all the drawers, chose a few pieces of furniture for herself and sold what was left. Then they all went back to the Registry Office.

Madame's armchair, her little table, her foot-warmer and the eight chairs had all gone! On the walls, yellow patches marked the places where pictures had once hung. They had taken away the children's beds, along with their mattresses, and the cupboard had been cleared of all Virginie's things. Félicité went from room to room, heartbroken.

The following day, a notice appeared on the front door. The apothecary shouted into Félicité's ear that the house was for sale.

Félicité's head began to swim and she had to sit down.

What most upset her was the thought of having to move out of her own room; it was the perfect place for poor Loulou. In her anguish she would gaze at him and beg the Holy Spirit to come to her aid. She developed the idolatrous habit of kneeling in front of the parrot to say her prayers. Sometimes the sun would catch the parrot's glass eye as it came through the little window, causing an emanation of radiant light that sent her into ecstasies.

Félicité had been left a pension of three hundred and eighty francs by her mistress. The garden provided her with vegetables. As for clothes, she had sufficient to last her her lifetime and she saved on lighting by going to bed as soon as it began to get dark.

She hardly ever went out, because she disliked walking past the secondhand dealer's shop, where some of the old furniture was on display. Ever since her fit of giddiness, she had been dragging one leg and, as she was now growing frail, old Madame Simon, whose grocery business had recently collapsed, used to come round every morning to chop her firewood and draw her water.

Her eyes grew weaker. The shutters were no longer opened. Many years passed. Nobody came to rent the house and nobody came to buy it.

Félicité never asked for any repairs to be done, because she was frightened she might be evicted. The laths in the roof rotted and for one whole winter her bolster was permanently wet from the rain. Shortly after Easter, she coughed blood.

Madame Simon called for a doctor. Félicité wanted to know what was wrong with her. But by now she was too deaf to hear what was said and she only managed to catch one word: 'pneumonia'. It was a word she knew and she quietly answered, 'Ah! Like Madame', finding it quite natural that she should follow in her mistress's footsteps.

The time for preparing the altars of repose was drawing near.

The first of them was always placed at the foot of the hill, the second outside the post office and the third about half-way up the street. The exact position of this last altar was a matter of some rivalry, but the women of the parish eventually agreed that it should be placed in Madame Aubain's courtyard.

Félicité's breathing was getting worse and she was becoming more feverish. She fretted at not being able to do anything for the altar. If only there were at least something that she could put on it! And then she thought of the parrot. The neighbours objected, saying that it was not really suitable. But the curé gave his permission and this made Félicité so happy that she asked him to accept Loulou, the one treasure she possessed, as a gift from her when she died.

From Tuesday to Saturday, the eve of Corpus Christi, her coughing increased. By the evening, her face looked drawn, her lips were sticking to her gums and she began vomiting. The following morning, at first light, feeling very low, she sent for a priest. Three good women stood round her as she was given extreme unction. She then announced that she needed to speak to Fabu.

Fabu arrived dressed in his Sunday best and feeling very ill at ease in such sombre surroundings.

'Please forgive me,' she said, summoning all her

strength to extend her arm towards him, 'I thought it was you who had killed him.'

What was all this nonsense? How could she suspect someone like him of having committed a murder! Fabu was most indignant and was on the point of losing his temper.

'Her mind is wandering,' they said. 'Surely you can see that.'

From time to time Félicité seemed to be speaking to phantoms. The women went away. Madame Simon ate her lunch.

A little later she went to fetch Loulou and held him close to Félicité. 'Come on,' she said. 'Say goodbye to him.'

Although Loulou was not a corpse, he was being eaten away by maggots. One of his wings was broken and the stuffing was coming out of his stomach. But Félicité was now blind. She kissed him on his forehead and held him against her cheek. Madame Simon took him from her and went to replace him on the altar.

5

The smells of summer drifted in from the meadows. The air was filled with the buzzing of flies. The sun glinted on the surface of the river and warmed the slates of the roof. Madame Simon had come back into the room and was gently nodding off to sleep.

She was awoken by the sound of bells; they were coming out of vespers. Félicité grew suddenly calmer. She thought of the procession and saw everything as clearly as if she were there.

All the schoolchildren, the choristers and the firemen were walking along the pavements. In the middle of the street, at the head of the procession, came the church officer with his halberd, the beadle carrying the great cross, the schoolmaster in charge of the boys and the nun keeping a motherly eye on the girls. Three of the prettiest, looking like curly headed angels, were throwing rose petals in the air. They were followed by the deacon conducting the band with arms outstretched and two censer-bearers turning round at every step to face the Holy Sacrament, which was carried by Monsieur le Curé, clad in his magnificent chasuble and protected by a canopy of bright red velvet held aloft by four churchwardens. A great throng of people followed on behind as the procession made its way between the white sheets which draped the walls of the houses and eventually arrived at the bottom of the hill.

Félicité's forehead was bathed in a cold sweat. Madame Simon sponged it with a cloth, telling herself that one day she would go the same way.

The noise of the crowd gradually increased, at one point becoming very loud and then fading away.

A sudden burst of gunfire rattled the window panes. The postilions were saluting the monstrance. Félicité rolled her eyes and, trying to raise her voice above a whisper, she asked, 'Is he all right?' She was still worrying about the parrot.

Félicité was now entering her final moments. Her breath came in short raucous gasps, making her sides heave. Beads of froth gathered in the corners of her mouth and her whole body began to shake.

From the street outside came the blaring of ophicleides, the high-pitched voices of the children and the deeper voices of the men. There were moments when all was quiet and all that could be heard was the tread of feet, cushioned by the scattered petals and sounding like a flock of sheep crossing a field.

The group of clergy entered the courtyard. Madame Simon climbed up on to a chair to look out of the little window and was able to see the altar directly below.

It was hung with green garlands and covered with a flounce in English point lace. Standing in the centre was a little square frame containing some relics and at each end there was an orange tree. Along the length of the altar there was a row of silver candlesticks and china vases containing a vivid display of sunflowers, lilies, peonies, foxgloves and bunches of hydrangea. A cascade of bright colours fell from the top of the altar down to the carpet spread out on the cobblestones beneath it. In amongst the flowers could be seen a number of other treasured ornaments: a silver-gilt sugar-bowl decorated with a ring of violets, a set of pendants cut from Alençon gemstones glittering on a little carpet of moss, two Chinese screens with painted landscapes. Loulou lay hidden beneath some roses and all that could be seen of him was the spot of blue on the top of his head, like a disc of lapis lazuli.

The churchwardens, the choristers and the children took up their places around three sides of the courtyard. The priest slowly walked up the steps and placed his great shining orb on the lace altar cloth. Everyone fell to their knees. There was a deep silence in which all that could be heard was the sound of the censers sliding on their chains as they were swung backwards and forwards.

A blue haze of incense floated up into Félicité's room. She opened her nostrils wide to breathe it in, savouring it with mystical fervour. Her eyes closed and a smile played on her lips. One by one her heartbeats became slower, growing successively weaker and fainter like a fountain running dry, an echo fading away. With her dying breath she imagined she saw a huge parrot hovering above her head as the heavens parted to receive her.